Slug in love

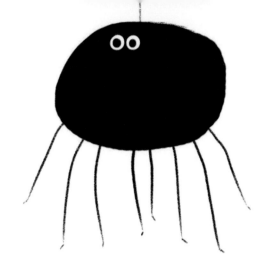

For the lovers and the huggers of
the world (and one in particular), Rx

For all the Gails . . .
N.S.

SIMON & SCHUSTER
First published in Great Britain in 2021 by Simon & Schuster UK Ltd • 1st Floor,
222 Gray's Inn Road, London, WC1X 8HB • Text copyright © 2021 Rachel Bright
Illustrations copyright © 2021 Nadia Shireen • The right of Rachel Bright and
Nadia Shireen to be identified as the author and illustrator of this work has been
asserted by them in accordance with the Copyright, Designs and Patents Act, 1988.
All rights reserved, including the right of reproduction in whole or in part in any form.
A CIP catalogue record for this book is available from the British Library upon request.
978-1-4711-8860-2 (HB) • 978-1-4711-8861-9 (PB) • 978-1-4711-8862-6 (eBook)
Printed in China • 10 9 8 7 6 5 4 3 2 1

Slug in love

RACHEL BRIGHT   NADIA SHIREEN

SIMON & SCHUSTER
London   New York   Sydney   Toronto   New Delhi

There goes Doug.
Doug is a **slug**.

Doug is a **slug** . . .

who needs a hug.

Hey, Doug!

Need a hug?

Yep.

Doug is a **slug**
in need of a hug.

But *who* wants to hug

a **slug** called Doug?

No one. That's who.

Not him.

Not me.

Not you.

Icky, mucky!

Yucky, sticky!

So on plods Doug . . .

poor **slug**.

But **wait!**

Here is a **snail**!

A **snail** called Gail.

SHE is grimy, slippy,
squelchy, slimy.

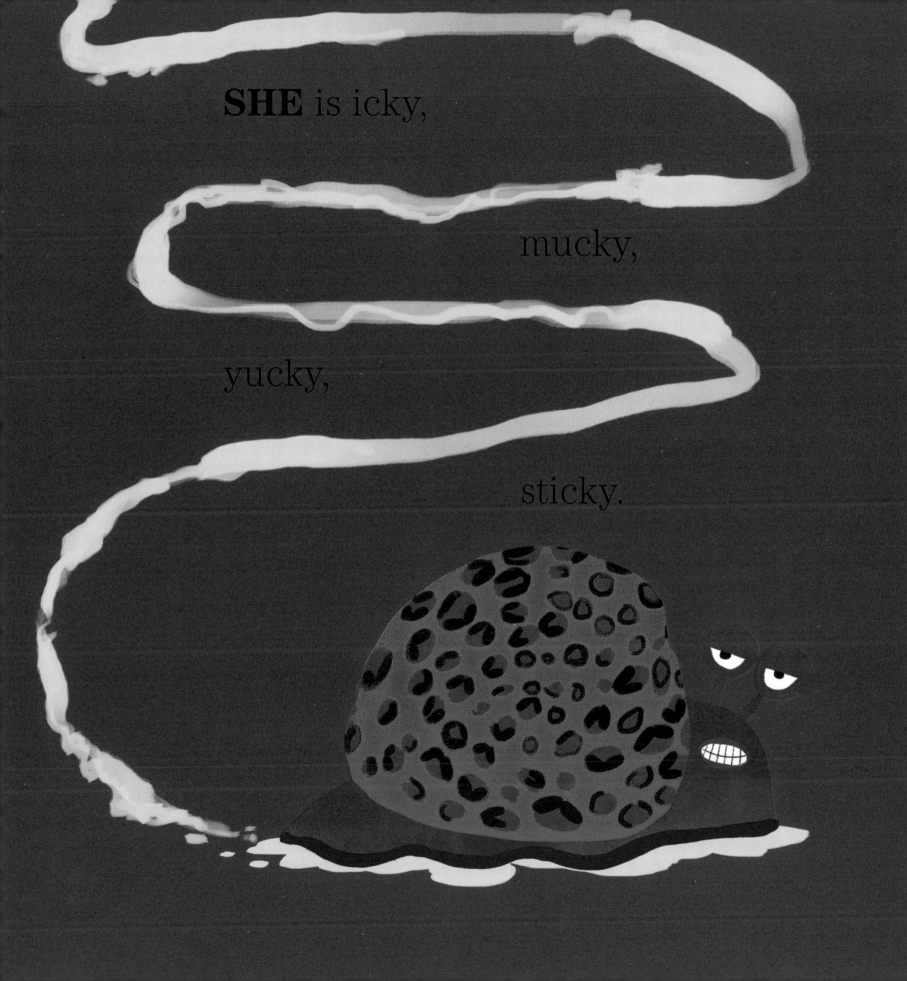

SHE is icky,

mucky,

yucky,

sticky.

She's THE ONE for lonely Doug!
Doug the **slug**
who needs a hug.

A **snail** like Gail?
It cannot fail!

"Errrrmmmm," says Doug.

"NOOOOO!" wails Gail.
It seems our master plan DID fail.

So on goes Doug,

our lonesome **slug**,

who's **never** going to get a hug . . .

Oh, Doug.

But . . . you never know

how, when or why,

some love might just come
flying by.

This is Doug.
He found his **bug**
and now he's super duper snug.

This is Doug.
He got his hug.
He is a **slug** . . .

. . . a **slug** in love.